# FACT CAT

# GRAINS AND CEREALS

Izzi Howell

WAYLAND
www.waylandbooks.co.uk

**FACT CAT**

**Get your paws on this fantastic new mega-series from Wayland!**

Join our Fact Cat on a journey of fun learning about every subject under the sun!

First published in Great Britain in 2017 by Wayland
Copyright © Hodder and Stoughton Limited, 2017

ISBN: 978 1 5263 0382 0
10 9 8 7 6 5 4 3 2 1

MIX
Paper from responsible sources
FSC® C104740

Wayland
An imprint of Hachette Children's Group
Part of Hodder & Stoughton
Carmelite House
50 Victoria Embankment
London EC4Y 0DZ

An Hachette UK Company
www.hachette.co.uk
www.hachettechildrens.co.uk

A catalogue for this title is available from the British Library
Printed and bound in China

Produced for Wayland by
White-Thomson Publishing Ltd
www.wtpub.co.uk

Editor: Izzi Howell
Design: Clare Nicholas
Fact Cat illustrations: Shutterstock/Julien Troneur
Other illustrations: Stefan Chabluk
Consultant: Karina Philip

The author, Izzi Howell, is a writer and editor specialising in children's educational publishing.

The consultant, Karina Philip, is a teacher and a primary literacy consultant with an MA in creative writing.

**FACT CAT FACT**

There is a question for you to answer on most spreads in this book. You can check your answers on page 24.

# CONTENTS

# WHAT ARE GRAINS AND CEREALS?

Grains and cereals are hard seeds that grow on plants. Cereals come from plants in the grass family.

Rice and wheat are cereals. Their seeds grow on the ends of stalks.

rice plant

wheat plant

Most people eat grains and cereals many times a day. You can eat dishes made from grains and cereals as part of a **balanced diet**.

People with coeliac (say see-lee-ac) disease can't eat **gluten**, which is found in wheat and barley. They have to eat grains that are gluten-free, such as rice.

Cornflakes are a breakfast food made from corn. Corn is a type of cereal. Which cereal is the breakfast food porridge made from?

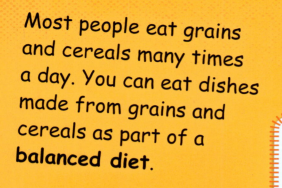

# RICE, WHEAT AND CORN

The cereals that we eat most often are rice, wheat and corn. Cooked grains of rice are eaten with many different **savoury** meals, such as curry. Wheat is usually made into flour.

Each grain of rice, wheat or corn is very small.

rice

wheat

corn

popcorn

These are some dishes that can be made from corn. How is corn turned into popcorn?

tortillas

Corn is a useful cereal. We can **grind** it into **cornmeal** and use it to make **tortillas**. Cornflakes are made from **toasted** corn. **Unripe** sweetcorn is eaten like a vegetable.

cornbread

# DIFFERENT CEREALS

This Indian farmer is growing millet. Millet is an important food in dry parts of Africa and Asia where other crops do not grow well.

Oats, barley and millet are different types of cereals. They aren't eaten as much as rice, wheat and corn. However, in some places, they are an important part of people's diets.

Oats grow well in cold areas, such as northern Europe. They are often added to biscuits and muesli. Barley is sometimes cooked in stews and soups.

In the United Kingdom, people eat oatcakes with cheese and chutney.

This is a beef and barley stew. Cooked barley has a chewy **texture**.

**FACT CAT FACT**

Barley, oats and most other grains are often fed to animals, such as cows and horses. Animals eat these grains in the winter when they can't eat grass.

# FARMING

Farmers plant grains and cereals in fields. They water the plants and **weed** the fields so that the plants have space to grow.

This farmer is planting rice. Some types of rice grow best in very wet fields. Find out the name of a country where they grow rice.

Grains and cereals are ready to be **harvested** after the plants die and turn brown. Today, most farmers use a combine harvester to harvest their crops.

Before combine harvesters were invented, people had to harvest crops by hand. They cut down the plants using big knives. Then they separated the grains themselves.

The combine harvester cuts down the plants. It also separates the grains from the rest of the plant. Then, the grains are poured into a big container.

separated grains

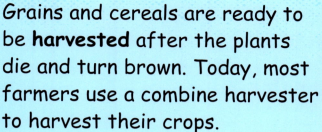

combine harvester

11

# COOKING

We need to cook most grains and cereals before we eat them. The easiest way to cook grains is to **boil** them in water until they get soft.

Grains of cooked rice are bigger than **raw** grains. Which of these bowls contains raw rice?

Always check with an adult before eating or cooking grains and cereals.

Cooked grains don't have a strong **flavour**. We add herbs and spices to them so that they taste nice.

Tabbouleh (say tab-oo-luh) is a Middle Eastern dish made from wheat. It contains lots of herbs, such as parsley and mint.

FACT CAT FACT

You can also make grains and cereals into desserts! Rice pudding is made by cooking rice with milk and sugar.

13

# FLOUR

We make flour from many types of grains and cereals, such as wheat, rice and corn. Machines grind the dried grains into a fine powder in factories.

In some parts of the world, people grind flour by hand. These Ethiopian women are using stones to grind the grains.

## FACT CAT FACT

Wholemeal flour is made by grinding **whole grains**. White flour is made by removing the outside part of grains and just grinding the insides.

Flour is used to make bread, pasta and noodles. Most bread is made from wheat flour. Some noodles are made from rice flour.

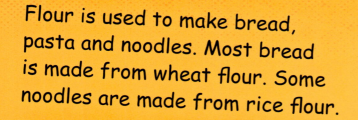

This person is using a machine to cut strips of pasta. The pasta **dough** is made from wheat flour, eggs and water.

# FIBRE AND CARBOHYDRATE

Food made from whole grains, such as wholemeal bread, contains **fibre**. Fibre helps your body to **digest** food.

Some types of wholemeal bread have seeds on top. The seeds add **protein** to the bread and give it a crunchy topping.

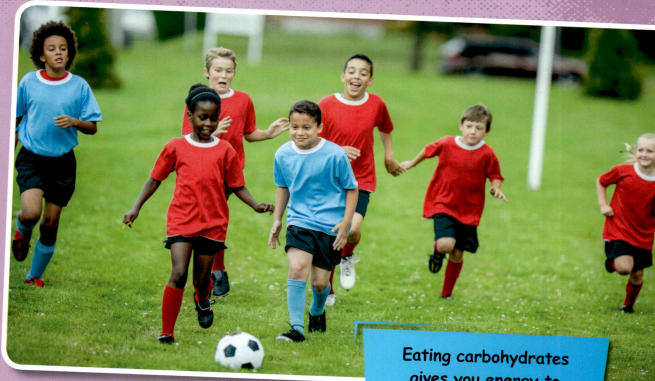

All grains and cereals contain **carbohydrates**. Carbohydrates give us energy. We need energy for our bodies to work and move around.

Eating carbohydrates gives you energy to play sports, such as football. Which yellow fruit contains lots of carbohydrates?

FACT CAT FACT

It's better to get carbohydrates from wholemeal bread than white bread. Your body quickly digests the carbohydrate in white bread. This makes you feel hungry soon after eating it. It takes longer to digest wholemeal bread, so you will have energy for longer.

# A BALANCED DIET

Eating food from different food groups will help you to have a balanced diet. Grains and cereals are an example of a food group.

This plate of chicken and vegetable stir-fry with rice contains food from three different food groups. Look at the chart on page 19 and name the three food groups in this dish.

This diagram shows you how much of each type of food you should eat. The large parts of the circle show foods you should eat at most meals. The small parts of the circle show foods you should eat less often.

Grains and cereals are in this part of the circle. You should eat them several times a day.

Fruit and vegetables

Grains and cereals

Meat, fish and eggs

Oil and butter

Dairy products

# AROUND THE WORLD

Grains and cereals are prepared in different ways around the world. For example, wheat is made into couscous in North Africa and pita bread in the Middle East.

In Italy, they eat polenta (cornmeal porridge) with meat stew.

Tamales from Central America are made by cooking cornmeal and meat inside a leaf. Which type of leaf do they use?

In some countries, they eat grains and cereals that can only be grown in their **local** area. Some of these grains have become popular in other countries as well.

This woman from Bolivia is harvesting quinoa (say keen-wah). Quinoa is a grain that grows on the high mountains of South America.

quinoa

**QUIZ** Try to answer the questions below. Look back through the book to help you. Check your answers on page 24.

**1** Cereals come from plants in the grass family. True or not true?

a) true

b) not true

**2** Which cereal are tortillas made from?

a) corn

b) rice

c) wheat

**3** Rice grows well in wet fields. True or not true?

a) true

b) not true

**4** What does fibre do?

a) give you energy

b) help you digest food

c) make your hair shiny

**5** It is better to get carbohydrates from white bread. True or not true?

a) true

b) not true

**6** Where does quinoa grow?

a) South America

b) Africa

c) Europe

# GLOSSARY

**balanced diet** a diet that has a healthy mixture of different foods

**boil** to cook something in very hot water

**carbohydrate** something found in food that gives your body energy

**cornmeal** flour made from corn

**crops** a fruit or vegetable that a farmer grows in large amounts

**digest** to use the food in your stomach as energy

**dough** a mixture of flour and liquid used to make bread and pasta

**fibre** something found in food that your body needs for digestion

**flavour** the taste of a food or drink

**fuel** something that is burned to give heat or power

**gluten** something found in wheat and barley that some people can't eat

**grind** to rub something until it becomes a powder

**harvest** to collect crops that are ready to eat

**local** describes something that comes from the area near you

**protein** something that is in food that helps the body to grow and be strong

**raw** not cooked

**savoury** a savoury dish is not sweet

**syrup** a sweet, sticky liquid

**texture** the way that something feels

**toasted** to heat something until it becomes brown

**tortilla** a corn pancake originally from Mexico

**unripe** describes a fruit or vegetable that isn't ready to be eaten

**USA** the United States of America

**weed** to take away plants that you do not want growing in an area

**whole grain** the grain including the outer layer

# INDEX

# ANSWERS

## Pages 4–20

**Page 5:** Oats

**Page 7:** Heat it up until it pops open.

**Page 10:** Some countries include India, China and Indonesia.

**Page 12:** The bowl at the top

**Page 17:** Banana

**Page 18:** Meat and fish, fruit and vegetables and grains and cereals.

**Page 20:** Corn or banana leaf

## Quiz answers

1    true

2    a - corn

3    true

4    b – help you digest food

5    not true – it is better to get carbohydrates from wholemeal bread.

6    a – South America

# OTHER TITLES IN THE FACT CAT SERIES...

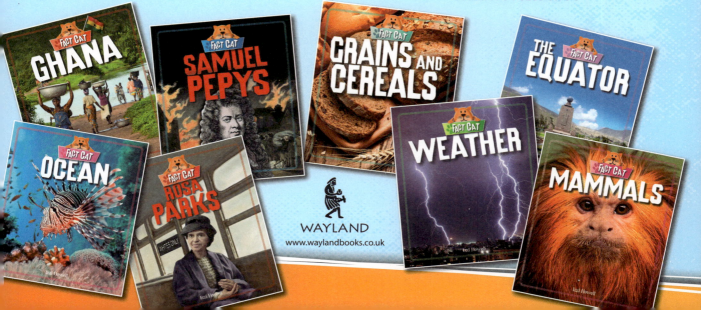

WAYLAND
www.waylandbooks.co.uk